KATE on the CASE

TRUMPET BERRIES

KATE on the CASE

The CALL OF THE SILVER WIBBLER

◦ HANNAH PECK ◦

Drumcondra Branch

Piccadilly
PRESS

First published in Great Britain in 2022 by
PICCADILLY PRESS
4th Floor, Victoria House, Bloomsbury Square
London WC1B 4DA
Owned by Bonnier Books
Sveavägen 56, Stockholm, Sweden
www.piccadillypress.co.uk

Text and illustrations
copyright © Hannah Peck, 2022

A CIP catalogue record for this book is available from the British Library.

ISBN: 978-1-80078-013-2
Also available as an ebook and in audio

1 3 5 7 9 10 8 6 4 3 2

Designed by Janene Spencer
Printed and bound in China

MIX
Paper from
responsible sources
FSC® C104723
www.fsc.org

Piccadilly Press is an imprint of Bonnier Books UK
www.bonnierbooks.co.uk

For Emmie and Sophie

FORMAL INTRODUCTIONS
— OUR CAST OF CHARACTERS —

KATE

OUR MAIN CHARACTER

SPECIAL-CORRESPONDENT-IN-TRAINING WITH ONE BIG STORY UNDER HER BELT.

BEST FRIEND OF RUPERT.

CURIOUS AND BRAVE.

SPECIAL CORRESPONDENT MANUAL

RUPERT
BEST FRIEND OF KATE, LOVER OF ROUSING SPEECHES.

KATE'S DAD
PROBABLY THE NICEST MAN

BIRD BRIGADER

NAME: BERYL

BIRD-BRIGADER WITH ONE BADGE IN PENCIL-SHARPENENING...

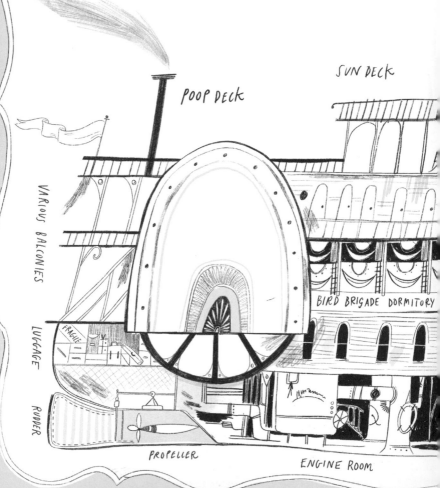

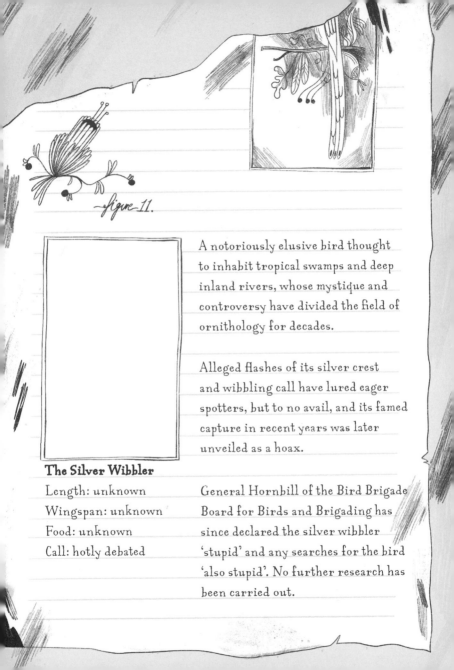

figure 11.

A notoriously elusive bird thought to inhabit tropical swamps and deep inland rivers, whose mystique and controversy have divided the field of ornithology for decades.

Alleged flashes of its silver crest and wibbling call have lured eager spotters, but to no avail, and its famed capture in recent years was later unveiled as a hoax.

The Silver Wibbler

Length: unknown
Wingspan: unknown
Food: unknown
Call: hotly debated

General Hornbill of the Bird Brigade Board for Birds and Brigading has since declared the silver wibbler 'stupid' and any searches for the bird 'also stupid'. No further research has been carried out.

CHAPTER ONE

Kate took a sip of her ice-cold apricot juice and looked out at the slowly passing jungle. She was on the poop deck – the very top deck – of *Miss Custard*, a fancy white steamboat that was chugging through green waters and giant glossy leaves on a special cruise in celebration of the Captain's new range of mayonnaise.

Along with her dad and her best friend Rupert, Kate was here to write

a food review for *The Lookout Post*
by commission of her One True Idol,
Catherine Rodríguez. It was a very
exciting job. Unfortunately, Kate was
finding it difficult. This was why:

MoRE SHRiiM

trilled Captain Mustard from overhead.
She was abseiling down the boat's huge
chimney, glittery trousers flapping, with a
steaming platter balanced on one hand.

Captain Mustard seemed to be
everywhere all at once, one second
springing up from behind a coil of oily
rope, the next swinging between open

balconies and plonking herself right into the seat next to Kate.

'You had better give me a good review now!' said Captain Mustard, handing over the wobbly shrimp. 'Not like those lies they spin in *The Daily Spoon*!'

'Of course,' said Kate, weakly. This time the shrimps were covered in a lurid orange sauce, and . . . holy moly . . . were those sprinkles?!

'I think I'm going to be sick again,'

said Rupert as soon as Captain Mustard had bounced away, globs of sauce splattering the deck behind her.

Rupert had been sick three times already. It probably didn't help that he was a strict vegetarian and kept staring deep into the eyes of the dead shrimps and saying things like, 'Do you think he had ever been in love?' or 'This one could have been an incredible artist. I can tell by the antennae.' It was getting very tedious, and Kate was struggling to write anything at all.

WITH COMPLIMENTS

CAPTAIN MUSTARD

CURRY

SHRIMP REVIEW No. 001

SPICY?

TOO SPICY

What Kate really wanted to do was open her *Special Correspondent Manual* and get stuck into a *proper* story. She wanted to write about the terrible evening entertainment (how had the singers got this job? Who agreed to make not one but *three* horrible dresses?), the jungle outside and how it made different noises at different times of day, and the troop of Bird Brigaders who carried clipboards and binoculars everywhere they went – even into the shower. (Kate knew this because Bertie, a friendly Bird Brigader, had told her so.)

The only thing getting in the way were these stinking shrimps. But she had promised Catherine Rodríguez she would get the job done, however boring it was, and she simply couldn't disappoint her hero.

A honking voice from the deck below interrupted Kate's pondering.

General Hornbill, the Bird Brigade leader, was stalking up and down a line of Bird Brigaders, who were all standing to rapt attention. He liked to talk an awful lot, and loudly too.

'If there's one thing that makes a top-ranking Bird Brigader, it's ORDER. I want boots polished, neckties steamed into isosceles triangles and the names of *every* living species of bird sewn into your sleeping bags in joined-up Latin!'

He stopped in front of a freckled

girl with a lot of fancy Bird Brigading badges. 'You!' He pointed at her. 'What is a parrot?'

'A vividly feathered bird with a hooked bill and rasping voice,' she recounted confidently.

'Good.'

'And you.' He peered down his beaky nose at Bertie. 'Recite for me, verbatim, the territorial call of the yellow-bellied ostrich.'

Bertie gulped nervously.

'AAAAAHHHAHHH?'

'WRONG!' General Hornbill barked over laughter from the rest of the brigade. 'Is there anything you *do* know, Bertrand Bimble?'

'Yes, actually!' Despite his reddening face, Bertie puffed out his chest. 'I know what the silver wibbler sounds like!'

General Hornbill snapped his head around. 'What?!' He stepped closer to Bertie. 'Did. You. Say?'

'That I know what th—'

'*There will be no utterance of that name while you are under my reluctant wing,*' the General hissed. 'Such a bird does not exist! It is nothing but a dreamer's dream, a fart in the wind, a myth for silly billies. And are *you* a silly billy, Bertie?'

Bertie looked at the floor and didn't say anything.

'I'm glad *I'm* not a Bird Brigader,' muttered Kate to Rupert. 'And who's got time for isosceles triangles?'

Not them, was the answer. Because it was exactly three o'clock.

'We promised Dad we wouldn't be late!' Kate scooped up Rupert and dashed down the metal steps onto the wide decking below, just in time to hear a wonky trombone lurch into parping song.

CHAPTER TWO

'Welcome to *Miss Custard*'s Condiment Cruise Bi-Annual Champion-Shrimps!' yodelled Captain Mustard, bursting out onto the deck through some gold curtains and making a deep bow to the crowd of passengers. 'Today we will be holding our first event in celebration of the good ship *Miss Custard*'s fiftieth year! FISHING!'

Dad, who was all trussed up in

galoshes, whooped and clapped very
loudly. He *loved* fishing!

'Whoever wins the most events will be
awarded a prize on the last day of our
cruise – a very *secret* prize.' The Captain
winked at the crowd. 'But for now . . .

ON–YOUR–SHARKS

GET–SET

GO!'

Captain Mustard waved a flag and everyone rushed to the jumbled pile of rods, snatching up the shiniest ones with the most colourful hooks first.

Squashed between General Hornbill's legs and a stranger's bottom, Kate grabbed the first thing she could.

'Oh dear,' she said to Rupert when the crowd parted. She was holding a crusty old cage that didn't look like it had caught anything in years, fish or otherwise.

Still, she swung it over the side,
hoping for at least a crab. A Special
Correspondent, *especially* if they were
in training, had to show capability at
every hurdle, even if it was fishing in a
ridiculous competition to commemorate
the Captain's new range of mayonnaise.

Soon fishing lines were whizzing
through the air along with shouts of 'I've
got one!', 'So close!' and 'GAAAAH!'

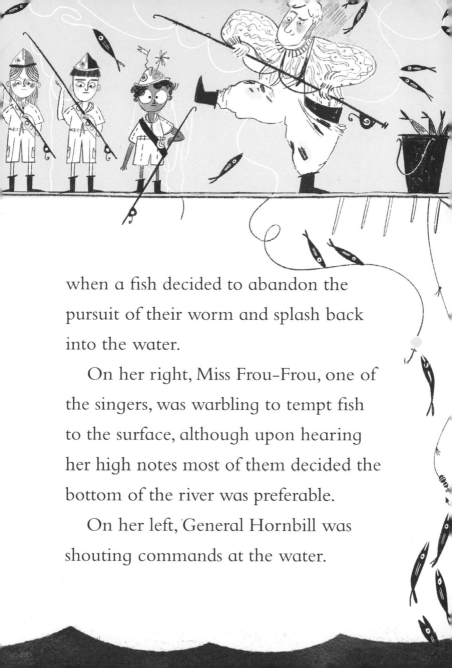

when a fish decided to abandon the
pursuit of their worm and splash back
into the water.

On her right, Miss Frou-Frou, one of
the singers, was warbling to tempt fish
to the surface, although upon hearing
her high notes most of them decided the
bottom of the river was preferable.

On her left, General Hornbill was
shouting commands at the water.

'Attention! ATTENTION!!'

'I suppose not everyone is aware he's a Very Important Bird Brigade General,' chuckled Rupert.

In fact, most of the fish were flocking to Dad, who was reeling them in like there was no tomorrow, no day after, no *nothing* except for fishing. His precision was incredible, his moves so slick, his mantra . . . well, you can decide for yourself.

And into the bucket fish happily plopped.

Kate had never seen him move so fast; his scores were soaring above everyone else's!

She abandoned her very unhelpful

and empty cage to watch and clap. Soon others started to gather around Dad's podium in awe. Everyone except the General, who, Kate noticed, had disappeared from the spot next to her, leaving behind an empty bucket. What a sore loser, she thought.

'DING!' hollered Captain Mustard. 'Your time is up! And we have our first winner!'

Everyone clapped while Captain Mustard pinned a large frilly rosette on Dad's galoshes.

'Well done, Dad!' said Kate. 'I wonder what you're on the way to winning!'

'Whatever it is, I hope it smells nicer than I do right now,' chortled Dad. 'And I haven't won yet, my little croissant!'

He was soon whisked away by fellow fishing enthusiasts keen to talk about tackles and reels and his impressive 'swish and swipe' technique.

'Kate, look!' It was Rupert, who was hauling their cage back onto the deck. 'We did catch something after all!'

And indeed they had. The something was wrapped in dripping water weed and vines, like a parcel delivered straight from the river. Kate tipped it out on the deck and carefully unwrapped it. Inside was a soggy book. It looked old.

'Forgotten treasures!' exclaimed Kate at the same time as Rupert squealed, 'Disgusting!'

'Oh, come on, Roo!'

'Don't wave that thing at me! It's covered in slime!'

'Just think – maybe it's full of secrets! Or from a lost jungle explorer! Or stuffed with maps! Or newspapers from hundreds of years ag—'

'*Someone's* looking for a story,' said Rupert with a mousy grin. 'But I suppose it's either this or more shrimps . . .'

CHAPTER THREE

After a quick and secret sandwich to avoid the never-ending supply of too-hot shrimp, Kate and Rupert scurried back to their cabin to inspect the book.

The pair had a tiny cabin all to themselves, with Dad's just next door. Everything was neat and tightly packed together. Mosquito nets and lanterns swung from the low ceiling, and a small round window looked out onto soupy green water and trailing vines.

Kate flopped onto her bunk and wiped some slime off the cover with a spare sock. It read:

The Diary of C. A. Bloom

[WORLD-FAMOUS BOTANIST, SCHOLAR of SPECTACULAR SPECIES]

ZOOLOGIST, ECOLOGIST, BIOLOGIST

'We get it,' muttered Rupert. 'You're very clever and you want us to know it.'

'Wait a minute!' Kate exclaimed, her hair fluffing up as it did when she was close to a good story. 'I know that name!'

Rupert's eyes narrowed the way they did when his walnut-sized brain was

contemplating enormous possibilities.
'It does sound rather familiar, doesn't it?'

'I guess there's only one way to find
out,' said Kate, and she opened the
soggy diary. It was crammed with
spindly handwriting and drawings
of peculiar-looking birds.

I have set up camp in this tropical perplexity.
The heat is unbearable. My ___ is blistering.
I am taunted by the titterings & toots of
undiscovered species, one of which I believe to
be the legendary silver wiffler, a bird so
shrouded in mystery one wonders if it might be
too hot in there, and won't it please come out?

I will not return home until it is in my
possession. My reputation as a botanist utterly
depends upon it!

Day 1

...only to catch a glance of it as it dashed away; a peculiarly grey tail and white wing bars, white eyes and a silver-spotted beak. I have never seen anything so beautiful—and yet so terrible—in all of my days. I must have it.

trackings - round 36

I am sure the Wibbler is taunting me. I woke to find a trail of green feathers placed on the ground. Upon following them I reached a note which read:

NICE TRY, SILLY BILLY

I believe the bird is not only literate, but *evil*

Day 110

I dare say the fecal matter left on my pillow is that of the Wibbler. I, on the other hand, have not defecated for days. The attacks are both smelly &

Day 145

I fear I am descending into frenzied...

'The silver wibbler!' cried Kate. 'That's the bird Bertie was talking about earlier!'

'I wonder if C. A. Bloom ever found it?' said Rupert.

'Whoever they are – a she or a he or a they – C. A. Bloom can't have,' said Kate, 'or else everyone would know about it – and Bird Brigade leaders like General Hornbill *especially*.'

'What were the chances of us fishing this out of the river . . . ?' mused Rupert, tapping his tail on the tip of his nose – but Kate was already miles ahead.

'Bertie would *worship* this book,' she continued. 'I bet we could help him decipher it and find out loads about the silver wibbler!'

'Kate . . .' said Rupert.

'Imagine if Bertie made the discovery! That would shut the General up once and for all!'

'*Kate*,' said Rupert.

'And then I could write an article about it and not have to do the shrimp stuff!'

'KATE!' said Rupert, heaving the heavy diary shut with his tail. 'That's exactly the problem – you've already got enough on your plate!'

'Oh, come on, Roo!' exclaimed Kate. 'You're as bored as I am! I've seen you playing chess against yourself behind the lifeboats! And remember last time – this could be our *second* big adventure!'

Rupert crossed his tiny arms. 'I nearly got eaten last time.'

'No, no – *we* nearly got eaten last time,' corrected Kate. 'But we didn't! We're still very much *not* eaten!'

The tiny arms stayed firmly folded.

'I'll let you listen to that tape of rousing speeches again . . .'

Rupert's ears twitched. He did love rousing speeches, it was true . . .

'And think about it – we could really help Bertie out,' pleaded Kate. 'A friendless misfit with one big dream . . .'

'Fine,' sighed Rupert.

Kate scooped him up and hugged him.

'And I want that sailor's hat from
the gift shop too,' he added in a muffled
squeak.

CHAPTER FOUR

Kate woke early the following morning – she wanted to give Bertie the diary before the Bird Brigaders began to recite their daily Bird Brigade promises and General Hornbill launched into his pre-breakfast speech.

She and Rupert found Bertie dangling his legs over the side of *Miss Custard*, the windmill on his hat whizzing furiously, but not as furiously as he was scribbling.

'Hi, Bertie! We've found something that might interest you!'

'Is it a one-way ticket off this boat?' said Bertie glumly, carrying on drawing.

'Not quite,' said Kate. She was about to change Bertie's whole day. 'In fact, it might make your time here *considerably more enjoyable*.'

Bertie perked up. 'What is it?'

'It's a book.'

'I don't like books.'

Inner gasp!

Kate was just trying to help! And who on earth didn't like books?!

'It's not just any old book!' she argued.

'I don't like books that aren't just any old books either,' snapped Bertie. 'I like no books at all a lot better!'

'But it's got some interesting informa—'

'Why does everyone think I'm STUPID!' Bertie shouted, throwing down his pencils. They clattered and scattered all over the place. A pair of passing polka-peppered parrots raised their eyebrows. 'Just because I only have two Bird Brigade badges and one of them is in pencil-sharpening doesn't mean I need your stupid book! Unless it's going to

help me impress General
Hornbill or find the silver wibbler,
LEAVE ME ALONE!'

'Bertie,' said Kate, 'it *IS* about the silver
wibbler! It's full of ways to catch it! It's
top-secret information!'

But before Bertie could respond, a
voice behind them made everyone jump.

'And what,' said General Hornbill, 'is
so worth knick-knacking about with
a non-Bird Brigader that you fail, yet
again, to attend the morning promises,
Bertrand Bimble?'

'Sorry, General Hornbill, I-I . . .'
stammered Bertie, but the General
ploughed on.

'You are one stripe away from zero.

And what happens when a Bird Brigader has zero stripes, Bertrand?'

'They can't be a Bird Brigader any more,' whispered Bertie.

'That's right,' said General Hornbill, solemnly. 'No birdseed for *you* today.'

'Is that what they eat?' whispered Rupert in shock.

Kate didn't answer. She was watching Bertie mope after the General, wiping his nose on his badge-less sleeve.

But just as he was about to go inside, he turned around and mouthed, 'The Bird Brigade dorm – tonight!
Bring the book!'

CHAPTER FIVE

Kate spent the rest of the day with Dad, who was steadily winning event after Champion-Shrimp event. He was first in the Chimney Shimmy, a race to the topmost point of *Miss Custard* with a hundred-year old barrel of mayonnaise strapped to his back; came first, second *and* third in Anchor Polishing; and was even lifted onto the shoulders of fellow competitors for completing the

Flying Flemish Five-strand – an infamous sailor's knot tied while the rope is airborne and thus requiring both juggling skills and sparklingly clear eyesight – in record time.

By afternoon he was covered in rosettes and telling anyone who would listen all about his 'swish and swipe' technique.

'I use it to take in the laundry, you see,' he would explain to admirers, and was so absorbed in describing every detail of the action that Kate was finding it very easy to avoid talking about shrimps and the work she wasn't doing.

It wasn't *her* fault shrimps were so boring, and she still had a few days to write something for Catherine Rodríguez – she just needed to make sure Bertie was okay first.

At last, it was dinner time. She told Dad that Rupert had been sick again and she needed to stay with him. The pair waited in her cabin until they were sure the corridors were empty.

'I wonder if Bertie's right about the silver wibbler after all,' mused Kate on the way. 'If there's someone else out there – a grown-up botanist too – who thinks it's real, surely he can't be completely wrong.'

'I don't know . . .' puffed Rupert, who had insisted on carrying the book himself. 'Sometimes people need stories to make life that little bit more sparkly.'

The Bird Brigade Dormitory was very
long and narrow, with hammocks lining
the walls, blankets folded and Bird
Brigading equipment organised to the
centimetre.

Bertie was the only one there and was
looking very much more cheerful than he
had been earlier.

'Have you got it?' he asked eagerly.

Kate handed the book over.

Bertie's eyes widened as he turned the
wrinkled pages. 'Flaming flamingos!' he
whispered. 'It's C. A. Bloom's diary!'

'You've heard of them?' asked Kate.

'*Heard* of him?' said Bertie, still
awestruck. 'No one else has ever got as

close to the silver wibbler as he did! He's legendary!'

'So he caught it?' asked Kate.

'Well,' said Bertie, lowering his voice to a nicely dramatic whisper – Kate had never seen him so animated, 'he was famously revealed to have faked his discovery of the wibbler.'

'So he lied?' said Rupert. 'Pretended he caught it?'

'Not exactly,' said Bertie, who was thoroughly enjoying himself. 'This is where it gets interesting. I don't think it was a hoax.

NOT.

AT.

All.'

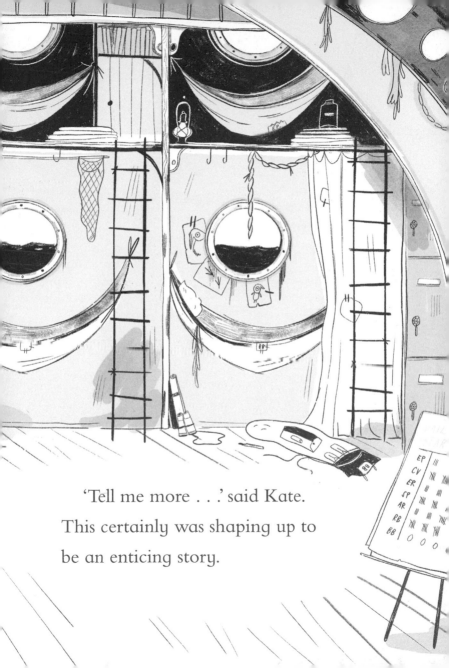

'Tell me more . . .' said Kate.
This certainly was shaping up to
be an enticing story.

'I think that C. A. Bloom was very close to getting the wibbler, but someone got in his way. Or set him up. Rumour has it he was close on its tail for months!'

'And so these —' Kate gestured to the book — 'were his findings?'

'Almost certainly,' said Bertie, flipping through the pages with wide eyes. 'And it's still legible too! C. A. Bloom was always renowned for his impeccable documenting and excellent spelling.'

'Was?' asked Rupert.

'No one has heard from him since The Hoax.'

'And we've found his diary!' exclaimed Kate. This was incredible!

'This part of the jungle is right

where he was looking,' said Bertie
enthusiastically. 'It's the only reason
I became a Bird Brigader in the first
place – I heard about the summer trip
here. Ever since The Hoax, I've been
obsessed with finding the silver wibbler.'

He sighed wistfully. 'They say it has the
most beautiful song in the whole world.'

Kate and Rupert nodded eagerly.

'And can shoot lasers out of its eyes,' Bertie added.

The pair exchanged a glance. A song, perhaps; lasers, no.

'Well,' said Kate, 'I'm in.'

'In what?' said Bertie.

'In on helping you find the silver wibbler, you crab stick!' said Kate. 'We're going to prove the General wrong!'

'I've got just one more question,' said Rupert in a very serious tone. 'Does General Hornbill *really* make you eat birdseed?'

CHAPTER SIX

The trio met in the Bird Brigade
Dormitory first thing the following
morning. After Bertie had initiated Kate
into the Bird Brigade, and Kate had
initiated Bertie into the ways of Special
Correspondenting, they got down to
business.

'First things first,' said Kate. 'We need
to find out exactly *how* C. A. Bloom got
so close to catching the silver wibbler, if

we're planning on doing the same.'

'Indeed.' Rupert nodded. He was considerably happier to help now that crisp white sailor's hat was perched between his ears.

Kate flipped open her tattered *Special Correspondent Manual* by her One True Idol, Catherine Rodríguez. Did it have anything to say about following a story into the depths of an unknown and potentially dangerous jungle?

Respect your Surroundings
Leave things as they are. Don't take anything unless it's absolutely necessary, especially if you're not supposed to be there.

SPEC

We all know reading a story can take you places, but what if writing one has you following a lead into a strange new environment?

TRACING YOUR STEPS

Mazes and string, forests and crumbs — you know the drill. Don't forget to plot where you've been so you can get out as quickly as possible if anything goes awry.

EXAMPLE

Cairo, Egypt - 2008.
In order to map my route through underground tunnels I drew a secret symbol on the walls each time I turned left.

'That's it!' declared Kate. 'We've got to make a map!' Could it be she was destined to become not only a Special Correspondent, but an explorer too?

Bertie beamed. 'I've sharpened my pencils especially.'

And so, with surprisingly effortless teamwork, they set about plotting C. A. Bloom's steps, scouring his diary for clues.

If you were to put your ear against the Bird Brigade Dormitory door, you would have heard – among the earnest sounds of scribbling and pen-tip chewing (and Bertie crying out as one burst and dribbled down his chin) – calls of 'left at the giant balancing rock', 'through the waterfall', 'do you think this says sticks or snakes?' and '*Other* left, Bertie!' as they created a map that would lead them straight into the wibbler's lair.

That night Kate, Rupert and Dad were all eating dinner under *Miss Custard*'s canopy. Dad's shrimps looked suspiciously more succulent than everyone else's, which Kate supposed had everything to do with the rosettes that were still pinned to his galoshes. Bertie was sitting at the Bird Brigaders' table, drawing pictures of the silver wibbler on his napkin and hiding it every time General Hornbill patrolled past. Miss Frou-Frou and her backing singers were warbling and Captain Mustard was whizzing around like a shrimp-flavoured firework, delivering steaming platters to everyone.

'And why haven't I seen my favourite girl-and-mouse double act up on deck today?' said Dad over his shrimp. 'If you're worried about sunburn, I have an *excellent* moisturiser.'

'It's not that, Dad,' said Kate, squirming in her seat. She should probably come clean; she always felt bad keeping things from him. 'We're actually, well . . . Rupert and I are working on a story right now.'

'Ah, the famous shrimp! You must be racing through that review, with the rate Captain Mustard is churning out dishes!'

Kate glanced guiltily at Rupert, who was poking a small piece of cheese with his fork.

'Well, it's actually something else – it's really interesting and if I could just –'

'Oh, Kate!' Dad whispered nervously. 'In any other circumstance you know I would be very excited for you. After all, my main aim is to be the most supportive father in the entire world, but . . .' He looked worried. 'But aren't you supposed to be writing for Catherine Rodríguez? It's the whole reason we're here. She didn't buy us the tickets for you to, well . . .'

Kate felt a strange mix of angry and sad, which didn't feel very nice. She wanted to impress Catherine Rodríguez, she really did! This was the woman who was singularly responsible for breaking at least twenty-six global scandals.

But it was getting harder and harder to focus when there was a brilliant story right under her nose. And what's more, *The Special Correspondent Manual* was proving to be much more help with her hunt for the silver wibbler than it was on rating shrimps.

'But, Dad, maybe Catherine will be more impressed with what I'm working on! She must have hired me for a reason – she said she liked my "perspective"!'

Dad opened his mouth. 'I think maybe –' But he was abruptly cut off by an eruption of noise from the next table. The Bird Brigade had launched into a chant so loud everyone else was staring. General Hornbill was conducting them with a spoon as they piled up their dirty plates in time to the words:

IS FOR BEING THE BEST (OF THE BEST!)

IS FOR IMAGINATION (DON'T USE IT!)

IS FOR BRIGADING SO HARD WE DON'T REST (NO!)

IS FOR DEHYDRATION (WE'RE FINE!)

Thank goodness. This horrible chant couldn't have come at a better time. 'Got to go, Dad!' said Kate, scooping up Rupert, who gave Dad an apologetic look, as she jumped down from her chair.

B IS FOR A BAITED TRAP TO CATCH THE ROMPING Rook

i IS FOR IMPECCABIE HANdWRITING IN OUR BIRd-BOOKS

G IS FOR THE GREEBY-SNEEB

A Nd ALL ITS FLAGRANT POMP. FOR the

D ABBLING DOVE WE TREK ACROSS THIS

E NDLESS SMELLY SWAMP!

CHAPTER SEVEN

Kate and Rupert were secretly
breakfasting on stolen shrimp free pastries
when the door to their cabin suddenly
flew open. Bertie stood panting, holding
a piece of paper out in front of him.

'C. A. Bloom found out the wibbler's
favourite food! Look!'
He thrust the
torn page at them.

Day 23

I have laid a selection of sandwiches outside camp in hope of luring the wibbler close. Tomorrow I will have insight into its dietary preferences.

Day 24

I awoke to a terrifying scene of destruction. The wibbler possesses _no_ sense of decorum (to be expected of any wild thing.) Every sandwich was left messily mangled, with only _ONE_ finished: The Trumpet berry baguette.

Although highly poisonous to humans, these rare berries appear to be the wibbler's 'Main Course' of choice. Furthermore, I have reason to believe the wibbler also pops these berries into 'cocktails' — the clink of glasses and hum of strange music can be heard in the night

'I can't believe we missed this!' exclaimed Rupert.

'No time to worry about that!' said Kate. 'We've got to get hold of some trumpetberries!'

'But how?' mused Rupert. 'We're on a moving boat . . .'

'And I've never even heard of them before! It's not like Captain Mustard is going to keep poisonous berries in the fridge –'

'I think I've got a plan,' interrupted Bertie, 'but it involves –' he gulped – 'thievery.'

'Bertie! Stealing is wrong!'

Rupert looked pointedly at the stolen breakfast spread out in front of them.

'I mean for Bertie it's wrong! He's got to keep his badges or else he'll be kicked out of the Bird Brigade!'

Bertie puffed himself up. 'But if we pull this off, I'll be the greatest Bird Brigader ever! The General keeps a whole stash of bird stuff in the bottom of the boat – he's got a locker down there and –'

'You think he might have some?' asked Kate.

'Yes. I think if there's any chance of finding some trumpetberries, it's down there.'

This was more like it! A story with a pinch of piracy was just what she needed. And they were on a boat too!

Drumcondra Branch

CHAPTER EIGHT

By this point in her career as a special correspondent, Kate knew a thing or two about sneaking and distractions, yessiree.

Together, Team Trumpetberry devised a daring and foolproof plan. Bertie would patrol the corridors to keep a lookout for General Hornbill, while Kate and Rupert went down into the creaky hull to steal the berries. If Bertie saw the General coming, he would drop his heavy backpack on the floor above them as a warning to scarper.

They would doubtless face all manner of obstacles down in the darkness – leaky pipes, unexpected rumblings, oil spills and, of course, locks.

Luckily for them, *The Special Correspondent Manual* had a whole chapter perfect for this very task. Surely Catherine Rodríguez would understand if Kate put her shrimp-sampling on hold when a better story came knocking . . . wouldn't she?

LOCK PICKING

There are many reasons one might need to pick a lock: to escape, to sneak, perhaps simply to experience the sheer adrenaline of it.* Not to be used lightly, this skill is one to be deployed in the most serious cases of Special Correspondenting.

The best way to pick a lock is with a special kit. However, anything pointy and thin will do. Search your pockets and the surrounding area. What do you see?

A pair of tweezers?

The back of an earring?

A spoon with an incredibly pliable and elegant handle?

Place your object inside the lock and

follow these steps:

1. INSERT OBJECT
2. CRANK
3. TWIST SEVEN TIMES
4. WAIT
5. OPEN
PROCEED WITH YOUR WITS ABOUT YOU.

*In your own home, of course.

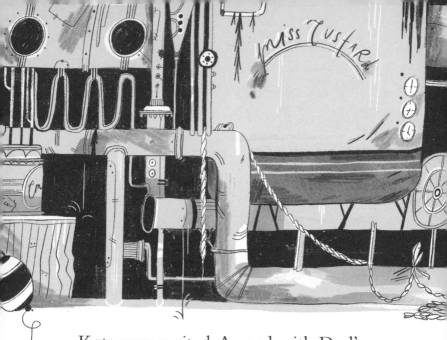

Kate was excited. Armed with Dad's tweezers (for Dad loved to keep a smooth nostril at all times) she and Rupert crept down into the belly of the boat, ready to pick any lock in their way.

'This is more like it!' Kate whispered as it got cold and clammy.

'I'll admit,' said Rupert, who was

leaping over puddles of slime, 'I've missed
sneaking with you.'

And sneak they did. They sneaked past
old tins of shrimp, ropes, lanterns, and
down a ladder into the clanking heart of
the boat. Steam hissed from rusting pipes,
and water dripped onto a large pile of
luggage.

'Nice to see everything is in full working order down here,' sniffed Rupert as he shimmied past an overflowing pile of dirty laundry.

'Oh, stop being such a snob,' said Kate. 'It's hard work running a boat. Anyway, no time to lose! Let's get searching.'

But they didn't have to search for long at all. Because there, right in front of them, inside General Hornbill's wide-open locker with a very clear label in capital letters were . . .

'Incredible!' said Bertie when they met him in the corridor, the berries safely tucked in Kate's pocket. 'That was the speediest heist I've been a part of!'

Kate didn't remind Bertie he'd never been part of a heist before. She was thinking. Something felt *off*.

'The locker was wide open!' reported Rupert. 'All we had to do was take them.'

'It was brilliant!' Kate beamed. 'We didn't even have to pick any locks!'

'Well, there was no one up on deck at all,' said Bertie excitedly. 'General Hornbill was doing an impromptu speech on the aerodynamics of a chicken. He didn't even notice I was gone!'

'Kate,' said Rupert that evening as they were snuggling down into their bunks after they had drawn at a game of cards. 'Do you think this silver wibbler business is all a bit *too* easy?'

'Pah! Weren't you listening at dinner?' Kate replied. 'Dad's giving me a really hard time about it.'

'But apart from that,' said Rupert, turning over in his sleeping sock. 'You know what I mean, Kate. The berries were just . . . lying there.'

Kate did know what he meant. But . . . 'Maybe things are just going well?' she reasoned. 'Not all stories have to be difficult.'

'This is true,' Rupert yawned. 'I

suppose I have a Mouse's Hunch, that's all.'

Kate knew that a Mouse's Hunch was a very powerful thing indeed, and not something Rupert would flap about willy-nilly. Rupert's great-aunt once had a Mouse's Hunch about Parmesan cheese, and a few days later a wheel of it had fallen down a ladder and flattened her.

Still, Kate thought, if she could pull this off she would impress Catherine

Rodríguez *and* help Bertie make one of the most important natural discoveries of all time, so there was no way she was going to sit around reviewing shrimp. That just wasn't the type of Special Correspondent she was.

CHAPTER NINE

After three evenings of secret scribbling,
spirits were high among the trio. The map
was looking as ready as it ever would,
they had the trumpetberries, and C. A.
Bloom was starting to feel more real to
them all, even though he did seem
a little old-fashioned
at times.

Day 156

In my watching & waiting I have lined up all my
apparatus alphabetically, polished every boot to
perfection. The wild around me threatens the very
tenets of civilisation, and so I, Clarence Adamar
Bloom, guardian, must remain it...

'I bet Clarence and General Hornbill would get on a treat!' commented Rupert.

'They do both love a well-folded sleeping-bag, don't they?' agreed Kate. 'Speaking of which, how are we doing with the list of things we need, Bertie?'

'Well,' said Bertie, scrambling to his feet, 'we need a net, jars, a camera, pencils

and paper, a torch, the trumpetberries –
we've got all those things already of
course – then . . . night goggles, a few big
sticks, some rope aaaand . . . a boat.'

A whole boat! Holy molluscs! How
could she have missed such a gaping hole
in their plan?

But she needn't have worried.

'I know!' chirped Rupert. 'There's an
old riverboat no one uses on the middle
deck. It's covered in a big canvas sheet.

It's called *The Shrimp Swindler*. I'm sure we can lower it down the side of *Miss Custard*.'

Kate scooped up Rupert and gave him a grateful squeeze.

'You're making my hat all wonky!' he protested, but he was smiling nonetheless.

Everything was coming together. All that was left to do was leave *Miss Custard* and venture out into the jungle. And what could possibly go wrong? They had advice from the best Special Correspondent in the world *and* from a very clever botanist, not to mention Bertie's drawing skills, Rupert's rousing speeches and Kate's direction.

Here was their plan:

CHAPTER TEN

They agreed to meet on the main deck
at midnight.

The moon was a big saucer of milk
in the inky sky, and all around were
the buzzings and rustlings of the jungle.
Somewhere out there, Kate thought, silver
wibblers were lurking, perhaps snuggling
down under a blanket in their treehouse,
or roasting a fish over a fire. Kate knew
Catherine Rodríguez would be proud of

her in this moment, shrimps or no shrimps.

'Pssst!' It was Bertie. He was sporting a pair of wobbly cardboard glasses and had a jar of fireflies tucked under his arm.

'Er . . .' said Kate, looking pointedly at the glasses. This operation had to be executed with slyness and stealth, and Bertie had all the grace of, well, a Bird Brigader in cardboard goggles.

'They're my night goggles!' said Bertie defensively. 'For seeing things! At night!'

Kate decided not to point out that her own lack of night goggles didn't seem to be a problem – there were more important things to attend to, like lowering *The Shrimp Swindler* into the waters below without a sound.

'Come on!' whispered Rupert. 'We need to get a move on!'

Like most of the things aboard *Miss Custard*, the riverboat was rusty, rickety and didn't look as if it could swindle anything, let alone shrimp. Still, the band bundled their provisions inside (taking special care with the trumpetberries) and began to lower *The Swindler* down the side of *Miss Custard*.

Although Kate was used to sneaking, stealing a whole boat was quite something. They lowered it past rows of balconies and life rings, past the kitchen, until it was swinging just outside the portholes of the Bird Brigade Dormitory. They were nearly there – a little bit more, and a bit to the left –

CRUUUUNK

The Shrimp Swindler swung dangerously, scraping the side of *Miss Custard* and hitting the water with a loud splash.

'I'm okay!' squeaked Rupert from below.

'Bertie!' hissed Kate. 'What's going on?'

'Oh, winking prawns!' cursed Bertie, scrambling for the rope he'd just dropped.

A light came on below them. There was no time!

'Drop the ropes!' shouted Kate. 'We have to jump! NOW!'

'I don't want to die!' yelled Bertie.

'Someone's at the window!' squealed Rupert.

There was *absolutely* nothing for it!

ONE...

TWO...

THREEe

CHAPTER ELEVEN

Kate opened her eyes. She definitely wasn't dead, which was excellent news. They had landed on the soft canopy of *The Swindler*, and Rupert had calmly taken the wheel beneath them and started the outboard motor. *Miss Custard* was far behind them – a fading star in the black.

'Bertie! What happened?' Kate asked as she brushed herself down. 'Why did you drop the rope?'

'I heard the silver wibbler!' said Bertie, who was straightening his cardboard glasses. 'Cross my heart! It was the song that was written in C. A. Bloom's diary too!'

'Holy mackerel,' Kate whispered. 'We must be on the right tracks!'

'Speaking of close calls,' said Rupert from below, 'we *may* have been spotted.'

'Did you see who it was?' asked Kate.

'I can't be too sure,' said Rupert, 'but I think it was a Bird Brigader. There were badges involved,' he added gravely.

Bertie shuddered. 'If it was General Hornbill, I'm birdseed. I might as well not go back.'

'Come on, Bertie!' said Kate. 'You

could be the one to finally catch the silver wibbler and become the best Bird Brigader of them all. I bet we're closer than we think. Pass me the map, Roo . . . See, we've passed the island that looks like a beak . . . those are the balancing rocks, just behind us . . .'

'I thought the balancing rock *was* the beaky island,' protested Bertie. 'They're exactly the same shape.'

'And look –' Rupert traced the tip of his tail along the dotted lines – 'we've passed this last landmark here, but none of the ones along the way – not the Venomous Vine Curtains, Red-Herring Rapids, or even the Curiously-Artistic-Carved-Log-Structure . . .'

'We're rubbish!' moaned Bertie, face in his hands. 'We're rubbish and we're lost!'

Kate couldn't believe it. They had studied C. A. Bloom's diary to the letter. One mistake was understandable, but this? It simply didn't make sense.

She remembered what Catherine Rodríguez had said about maps – knowing where you had come from was just as important as knowing where you were headed. Kate took out her trusty pencil and began scribbling over the map, redrawing their route.

They were not rubbish, nor lost. She was just lining up her compass when the water around *The Swindler* started to bubble.

'W–what's going on?' said Bertie.

Kate shone her trusty torch over the edge of the boat. The bubbles were getting bigger, frothing and gurgling and causing the boat to rock from side to side. But what was that? A faint greenish glow was appearing from the depths of the water. Kate ducked just in the nick of time.

EEEEEEEEEEEEEEEEEEEE!

A vivid green stream of slime erupted out of the water and landed with a heavy slap on the deck. More and more followed, wriggling and twisting in a giant knot of . . .

RIVER SNAKES!

In two seconds, they were everywhere. One knocked over the jar of fireflies

and sent
them flitting out into the
dark, another was gleefully
spinning the wheel with its
tail, sending the old boat churning in
mad circles.

'GET IT OFF ME!' shouted Bertie. A
particularly luminous snake was winding
itself about his leg, and had its jaws
clamped around his Bird Brigade sash.

Kate scooped up Rupert – dodging a

whizzing snake as
she did so – and lunged for
a fishing rod.

'Dad's fishing technique! What was
it again, Rupert?!'

'The swish and swipe!' he squealed
from her pocket.
'KATE! SNAKE! TWO
O'CLOCK!'

'SWISH, SWIPE,
SURRENDER,
THEN SEIZE!'

It was working! The snakes were darting towards the colourful fishing hooks instead of at them! Soon Kate was flinging them off the boat and into the water, where they landed with satisfying plops. There was just one more to go when –

'The berries!' yelled Bertie.

Kate spun around and saw the precious jar bouncing across the deck – it was nearly in the river, but then –

A claw stopped it.

A claw that was attached to a long, scaly leg, green-and-white striped feathers and a pointy beak. The silkiest of bandanas framed its beady eyes.

'Stand and deliver!' whooped the bird. 'Your nets or your *necks*!'

CHAPTER TWELVE

'Drop your weapon.'

'This isn't a weapon!' protested Kate.
'We —'

'Well, it sure looks like one to us,
slap-jack.'

Kate didn't have any other options. She
dropped the fishing rod. Two more birds
swooped aboard and began stuffing the
friends' possessions into swag bags. One
was silver with spangled, glittering wings,

and the other looked very much like a large feathered blueberry.

Both were wearing silky bandanas.

'Tie them up, Toot!' instructed the long-legged green bird.

'TOOOOT,' went the flying blueberry, and zoomed around the children with a rope.

'Look at this!' said the glittery bird, fingering the boat's tattered canopy. 'They've called themselves the Swindlers! Here to snatch us and shamelessly stuff us all into jars, are you?'

Kate groaned – this looked *terrible*.

'We're not here to swindle at all!' said Bertie. 'We just want to find – Ow!'

Kate had given him a hard pinch on

the arm. He mustn't say anything about the silver wibbler – who knew what these birds would do to them!

'What's that, you tittering toothpick?' said the green bird.

'N-nothing, sir – or is it madam?'

The bird hooted. 'We don't do that stuff, us birds.'

Kate could see that the berries were now firmly tucked into the silver bird's sack. They were about as far away from the wibbler as Captain Mustard was from changing her menu, and, as the glittery bird took the boat's wheel and turned them around, they were soon plunging even further into the dark unknown, totally and utterly kidnapped.

CHAPTER THIRTEEN

The vines were getting lower, the river thinner and the tree trunks thicker. As the boat chugged into the heart of the jungle, the birds began to chant.

'We loot and we toot, yes we're absolutely
    fruity
We'll kick you in the booty, we'll snatch
    away your snooty
We'll leave you wearing nothing but your
    nakey-birthday-suit-y

And that's when you'll know we're
the biiiiirds!

We protect, we respect, every neck-fleck-
speckled-peck
We pillage all the pillagers then leave
their boats to wreck
If we spy you with your nets, let it be
known
we'll have your necks
And that's when you'll know we're the
biiiiirds!'

'We get it!' muttered Rupert, who was
squashed between Kate and Bertie, tiny
legs dangling in the air.

But Kate wasn't in the mood for

biting observations. For the first time in her short but nonetheless brimmingly full-and-promising life, she was out of plans. When she had come face to face with a tiger at least she had been able to bargain with him. But these birds were different. They were wild, mean and didn't seem to need anything from her at all.

For the millionth time, Kate wondered what Catherine Rodríguez would do. But her One True Idol was too clever to get captured by looting birds, she thought glumly. If she had only followed orders and stuck to the shrimp story, she would never have wound up in such a mess.

Meanwhile, Toot was gearing up for his solo verse.

'Take it away, Toot!' hollered the long-legged green bird.

'TOOTY TOOT TOOTY TOOT,
　　TOOTY TOOTY TOOTY TOOTY
TOOT TOOTY TOOT TOOT
　　TOOTY TOOT TOOT TOOOOT
TOOTY TOOT, TOOTY TOOT,
　　TOOTY TOOTY TOOTY TOOTY
TOOT-TOOT TOOTY TOOTY
　　TOOTY TOOOOOOOOOOT!'

After what seemed like hours (and seven more painful renditions of Toot's solo), the vines began to part and a shadowy structure jutted up from the river.

It first appeared as some sort of

wrecked ship, then a crumbling castle, but, as the moon threw a beam of light through the trees, Kate saw nests balanced atop winding branches and ripped flags fluttering slowly in the dense jungle air. It was a treehouse.

'Flaming flamingos,' whispered Bertie in awe.

'What's that, kid? You wanna set some flamingos ablaze now?' said the green bird, who was lazily whittling a stick into the shape of a pineapple. 'Turn them pink wings into tasty bar-bee-cue dippers?'

'No!' gasped Bertie. 'No not at all I-I –'

'Better save your chatter for the interrogation.'

Kate gulped. She could feel Rupert

shivering behind her. 'You mean we've not even started the interrogation yet?'

'That's right, moo-moo. You can't expect to be shimmying round these parts with no complications. You know what they say . . .'

'Not really,' said Kate.

The bird looked at her with a sly smile. 'If you climb in the saddle, best be ready for the ride.'

CHAPTER FOURTEEN

The Swindlers were frogmarched down a wooden gangway and through a heavily bolted door. Once inside, Kate gasped – it was some sort of lawless library, but instead of books on shelves the whole place was crammed with *things*.

A chandelier of spoons swung from the sloping ceiling, telescopes, nets, arrow heads and compasses spilled out of crooked nests on shelves that went higher

and higher until Kate's neck started
to strain. She saw strange instruments
made of frying pans and washing line,
patchwork parachutes and mosquito nets
hanging from wonky wooden beams. If
she wasn't so kidnapped she would have
been completely awestruck.

The green bird started to walk around them. 'And what would three little critters like yourselves be doing jimmying about in our parts?'

'Um, just going for a night-time . . . drive?' said Kate. 'But we got lost.'

'You wouldn't be lugging your pudding feet in any particular direction?'

Kate could feel Rupert getting annoyed beside her. He was very sensitive about his feet.

'No . . .' lied Kate. 'Not at all.'

But the bird could tell she was lying, she was sure of it.

'You wouldn't be . . . *bottomists*?'

Rupert let out a squeak of laughter, which Kate hastily covered with a cough.

'Do you mean botanists?' asked Bertie innocently. Kate trod on his foot.

The green bird's eyes narrowed. 'That's what I said.'

'Yes, yes, that's what we mean, but no, we're not . . . um . . . bottomists,' said Kate.

'Righty-malighty,' said the glittering bird. 'And so if you're *not* bottomists, what are you doing with *these?*'

The trumpetberries!

'These nummy berries are very special to us birds. But we think you already know that. The last time we saw these delicious morsels we were being wrongfully, rude-fully, un-in-justifiably HUNTED.'

'We don't know what you're —'

'We're just . . . we . . . they . . .' stammered Kate.

'We're so sorry!' cried Bertie. 'We shouldn't have come here at all!'

The long-legged bird stopped its stalking circles and looked straight at Bertie.

'More of that, please.'

'We wanted to find a rare bird called the silver wibbler — perhaps you've heard of it?'

The bird didn't answer directly. 'And

why did you want to find this . . . silver wibbler?'

'B-because no one ever has before! Because I just wanted to be good at *something* – to impress General Hornbill! And I made two really good friends along the way, and now – sob sob . . . I just wanted to be the hero for *once*!'

Martha-mother-of-crisps! thought Kate. She would have to call him 'Blurtie' from now on – at least, if there *was* a 'from now on' from now on at all.

The bird took a long, hard look at Bertie's blotchy face.

'You wanna be a *real* hero, kid?'

He sniffed and nodded.

'You gotta know the trees, know the

slow groove of the river. Know which way is up and which way is down.'

'I know which way is up!' protested Bertie, wiping his tears. 'Up is up!' He paused. 'But then – oh no. Is it down . . . ?'

'Oh, Bertie,' sighed the bird. 'Sweet, condensed-milk-toothed Bertie. We all think we know what's up, but let me ask you this . . . You ever worn a snake like a silk scarf and danced naked under the bobbing moon?'

Bertie shook his head.

'You ever stuck googly eyes on your caboose and then waggled it over the precipice of a waterfall at passing day trippers just . . . because . . . you . . . could?'

Bertie shook his head again.

'These examples are worryingly specific . . .' whispered Kate to Rupert, who was almost as mesmerised as Bertie. 'You ever skiddley-da-da-dooed all over the pillow of a scrimpy, parrot-pinchin', tree-shimmying, microscope man?'

'Wait a minute!' interrupted Kate. 'Are you talking about –'

But the cool bird kept on talking, their eyes never leaving Bertie's.

'You ever told someone mean
they
    are a
        silly
            billy . . . ?'

'Wait *another* minute!' gasped Bertie.

And in the sudden way things often
come together, it all made perfect
sense to Kate. The tauntings C. A.
Bloom had written about, the green-
and-white plumage, the looting of
explorers' possessions –

'YOU'RE ThE SiLVER WiBBlER!'

CHAPTER FIFTEEN

Kate knew she was right! They *had* found what they were looking for – or perhaps it was the other way round.

For the first time, the birds fell silent.

'You've been playing tricks on explorers this whole time!

Luring them out here, making them delirious, stealing their things!' Kate was getting more confident.

'And all the while, there is no silver wibbler — at least, not really! *That's* the secret of the silver wibbler — that there isn't one at all!'

Rupert gasped. Bertie looked as if he was going to faint from the shock of it all.

'Well rattle my ribs and call me a radish,' said the long-legged green bird slowly, casually flicking a firefly off its wing. 'You sure are a smart one, girlie. You're ding-dang right, *but* —' it looked her dead in the eye — 'can you blame us?'

'I mean, I like a devious prank as much as the next precocious child,' reasoned Kate, 'but haven't you taken it a bit far . . . ? Stealing all our things and —'

The bird erupted into caws and cackles. 'OH, HOOO HOOOO! Let me tell you something. We're just your average brood of humble-drum jungle birds. Regular as pigeons, really.'

'But more stylish,' interrupted the silver bird.

'That's us. We got a certain feathery flair. But once people came sneaking about, poking our bums with their telescopers and micro-mobiles and

trying to make us eat tuna sandwiches like dafty duckies in a pond so that they could package us up into boxes, we wasn't going to sit on our wings and do nothing to defend ourselves.'

Kate paused. Here she was in the middle of an unknown and unplotted jungle, tied up in slimy rope by three bird-bandits, with no chance of escape. And she couldn't blame them. Not one bit.

'I don't blame you,' said Kate.

'A-and, and neither do I!' said Bertie, his voice wavering. 'I want to be a better explorer than C. A. Bloom. I don't want to put you in a box *or* poke your bum with a telescope!'

For the first time, the green bird broke into a smile. Its long wings shone in the moonlight. It looked strange, spectacular and wild.

'Loose the gooses,' it instructed the others, who, in a flash, slashed the rope from around the Swindlers.

Kate couldn't believe it!

'We're free!' gasped Bertie, as Toot and the silver bird slid the swag back towards them.

'Lucky you,' said the silver bird.

'Use your freedom wisely,' said the green bird. 'If you so much as whisper our secret in your sleep, we'll be on you like a leech in a jacuzzi.'

'Toot,' agreed Toot.

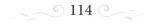

'My lips are sealed!' said Bertie eagerly. 'I don't want to swindle or swipe any more! As soon as we get back I'm going to break all my jars and rip up all my bird books and –'

'Boy,' interrupted the green bird, 'you wanna be a real hero?'

Bertie nodded.

'Then quit your terrarium living. Wake the wild within you! Waggle that caboose. Learn to say, "No, SIR"!'

And with that . . .

CHAPTER SIXTEEN

Sunlight streamed through the twisting vines and giant trees, warming the newly freed Swindlers. Flowers so big Kate could have sat in them bloomed overheard, and the cacklings and croonings she'd been so scared of last night sounded musical now she was among them, not listening from the deck of *Miss Custard*.

'That felt like a dream,' said Kate.

'More like a nightmare,' said Rupert. His sailor's hat had vanished and he was telling anyone who would listen that Toot had been 'eyeing it up', but Kate knew he was just as astonished by the night's events as herself and Bertie.

Bertie, mind you, had a smile so big it wasn't fading, and kept saying things like, 'Quit your terrarium living,' to Kate and, 'Keep driving, kid,' to Rupert.

As for Kate, she couldn't believe they'd done it. They were the only people in the world who knew the real story behind the silver wibbler. She felt a bit sorry for C. A. Bloom, who would never discover what it truly meant to be wild and free, or talk face to face with the three bandana-wearing birds who had fooled him so expertly. She wondered if he was still captivated by the birds, or if the diary they had studied was one of his last.

They rounded a corner and saw *Miss Custard* bobbing in the morning sun. Soon they were right beside her. Carefully and quietly, the gang tied *The Swindler* to her side, hurried up a ladder and tumbled aboard. On the deck above them, passengers were preparing for the Champion-Shrimp Awards.

'You know what, Rupert?' said Kate, straightening up. 'Maybe I should write about the shrimps and *Miss Custard* after all. I can report on the competition and how Dad wiped the floor with everyone.'

'And I've got a new-found confidence and relationship with our incredible environment that I want to share with all the Bird Brigaders and General Hornbill,' reeled off Bertie, his windmill hat spinning happily.

'*Do* you now?' The General was standing behind them, with a curious look in his eye that Kate couldn't quite read. But he kept talking before they could answer, his words getting faster and faster. 'You've been out! You've been off the boat and I know exactly why!

Empty your pockets, all of you!'

Kate was suddenly very aware of the map tucked in her top pocket. It led straight to the birds' secret lair – but hadn't General Hornbill made it exceedingly clear that the silver wibbler was a 'fart in the wind' and a 'myth for silly billies'?

'It's none of your business!' she retorted. He might have the right to boss Bertie around, but *she* wasn't a Bird Brigade!

'Oh, it's *all* of my business,' frothed the General, who was practically hopping. 'Tell me where it was! What does it look like? What is its wingspan?!'

Kate's mind was whizzing like a river snake. 'Are you talking about –'

'THE SILVER WIBBLER!' General Hornbill howled. 'I must have it! And *you* are about to show me how!'

'RUN!' yelled Kate. She didn't know what was going on, but she wasn't about to let the General get his hands on their map! Before she could scoop up Rupert and make a dash for it, the General snatched an oar from the floor, broke it clean in two over his knee and launched the pieces, spinning, through the air.

CHAPTER SEVENTEEN

The gang stumbled backwards and over
a tactically placed, combat-booted foot,
and BAM, before they knew it, they were
tumbling through an open door behind
them and into a cupboard and a pile of
Captain Mustard's gloopy galoshes.

'And now it's time to finish what I
started all those years ago!' brayed the
General, plucking the map from Kate's
pocket in a second, and then

tipping a basket of dirty laundry over them. 'And the best thing of all? You'll have led me straight there!'

'But you think the silver wibbler is a lie!' protested Kate, struggling to lift herself out from underneath some wet trousers.

'We're the ones who wanted to find it!'

'And why, you *disgusting conglomeration of bacteria*, do you think that is?' crooned General Hornbill. 'I'll tell you why! You have fallen straight into my trap! My perfect, precise, decisive, rigorous master plan! You think you found the silver wibbler all by yourself?! WRONG! Who planted the diary in your net at the fishing competition? ME! Who left the trumpet berries in plain sight, waiting to be pinched by three little creatures desperate for an adventure? ME AGAIN! ME, ME, ME – CLARENCE ADAMARIS BLOOM!'

Kate went red. Bertie went pale. Rupert's eyes bulged in a way that a mouse's eyes never should.

General Hornbill continued his horribly gleeful speech, his words getting faster and faster. 'I knew that a nosy little girl like you would be perfect for the task – you couldn't help yourself, with your desperate thirst for sneaking and flagrant disregard for authority!'

'You'll never find the silver wibbler!' cried a muffled Bertie from underneath a pair of wellies. 'It's cleverer than you!'

'Not any more!' snapped the General. 'Today will be the day I finally end its haunting tauntings and banish its shadowy wing from my dreams. I'll dart its little head stiff and stuff it into a glass box.'

And with that, he produced a key from a special pocket-inside-another-pocket, did a strange little dance on his tiptoes and slammed the cupboard door shut, locking it behind him.

CHAPTER EIGHTEEN

Slowly the Swindlers began to detangle
themselves from the pile of filthy laundry.
Rupert's white fur was all green and
sludgy and Bertie's windmill had been
sliced clean off by the spinning pieces
of oar.

Kate felt sick to her stomach. So General
Hornbill was C. A. Bloom. And with the
map — the map *she* had corrected — he
would reach their lair in no time.

The birds had trusted them, and look what had happened. They were clever and daring, but would they be able to hold their own against C. A. Bloom? Especially a C. A. Bloom brimming with rage and vengeance.

Rupert came and slumped next to her. Usually he would sneak under doors and unlock them from the outside, but boat doors were trickier than other doors.

'Bertie, why aren't you slumping?' asked Kate.

But Bertie wasn't listening.

'Now's not the time for sharpening pencils, Bertie!'

'Oh, ISN'T IT?' Bertie turned around.

Kate gasped. He was holding an exemplary sharpened pencil. The point was long and thin – perfect for lock-picking.

'I knew my Pencil Sharpening skills would come in handy one day!'

'Incredible!' said Kate and Rupert together. And it was. With a wiggle and a click they all burst out of the laundry cupboard and onto the empty deck. Parping music was drifting down from the deck above.

There was no time to lose! Now he had the map, the General would be off the boat and

making his way to the birds' secret lair immediately.

'He's headed for the poop deck!' cried Kate. 'Let's get that map!'

ChAPTER NINETEEN

They sprinted up the stairs, rounded
a corner and almost collided with
a shrimp-laden waiter. Apologising
hastily, they looked around. The deck
was brimming with white balloons and
parasols, crisp tablecloths and fluttering
flags. Subtle jazz was playing. Everyone
was dressed up in their best
frills and saying things like 'How
charming' and 'Sugared Shrimp?'

How were they supposed to find C. A.
Bloom in this maze of frills and confetti?

'We need to split up,' commanded
Kate. 'Roo, take the tables; Bertie, block
the railings with rope or something.' She
glanced around her and saw a platform
with a microphone stand. 'I'll head up
there for a better view. *Go!*'

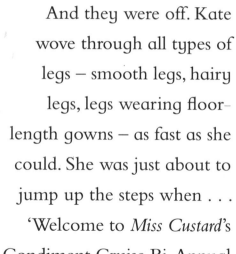

And they were off. Kate
wove through all types of
legs – smooth legs, hairy
legs, legs wearing floor-
length gowns – as fast as she
could. She was just about to
jump up the steps when . . .
'Welcome to *Miss Custard*'s
Condiment Cruise Bi-Annual

Champion-Shrimps Awards Ceremony!'
sang Captain Mustard, who had sprung
up from nowhere and was now in front
of the microphone. She was dressed to the
tens – this was the most important day of
the year for her. 'It's time to announce the
Grand Winner!'

Molluscs! Kate couldn't get on the
podium now! She strained above the
crowd and caught sight of Rupert
jumping up and down and waving at her
from atop a huge pile of steamed fish.
His tail was pointing at a dark head
moving towards the stern.

C. A. Bloom!

He was getting away! Kate could see Bertie struggling against the tide of happy passengers making their way to the podium. He would never reach C. A. Bloom in time, and, even if he did, what could he do once he got there?

Above her, Captain Mustard was gaining momentum. '. . . One of the most outstanding fishermen I have ever seen . . .'

Kate looked around in desperation. And then she saw it. A red envelope sitting on a small shiny table. A red envelope that said 'WINNER' on the front.

Quick as a snake she dashed over and tore it open. Inside was a piece of paper that read:

Oh no. This was certainly a horrible conundrum to be in. But she had to do *something*.

'A man whose dedication to facial moisturiser is truly an inspiration . . .' continued the Captain.

With her heart in her mouth, Kate scribbled out Dad's name and wrote another in its place, replacing it all just seconds before Captain Mustard reached for the envelope and read out . . .

'GENERAL HORNBILL?!'

The Captain was dumbfounded.

'He's over THERE!' Kate yelled,
pointing straight at him. The crowd
parted, revealing the dazed winner,
who was frozen to the spot with a map
between his teeth, and a backpack stuffed
full of terrible bird-catching traps.

Before he could so much as blink,

confetti was raining down on C. A. Bloom,
a marching band honked its way over,
plucked him off the railings and plonked
him onto their shoulders, all to the
cheering of the crowd.

'Brilliant!' Kate shouted to Rupert over
the whoops and claps. 'He can't escape
now!'

'A few words from our esteemed

winner?' asked Captain Mustard into the microphone, looking suspiciously at the slip of paper in her hands.

But for the first time in his life, words had failed Clarence Adamaris Bloom. Or perhaps he had failed them.

'*I'll* say a few words!' said a voice in the crowd.

Kate gasped.

It was *Bertie*.

General Hornbill paled. 'Don't listen to that poor excuse for a Bird Brigader. He's – he's hallucinating! He's having a reaction to Common Nightshade!'

The crowd gasped.

'YOU'RE a reaction to Common Nightshade!'

Bertie was standing tall on a table, dripping slime and mud all over the white cloth and paper napkins. The midday sun was behind him, and even though his declaration didn't make any sense, he looked the bravest Kate had ever seen him.

The crowd *OOOOHed*. They were very much enjoying this scandalous altercation.

'General Hornbill's been trying to catch the silver wibbler and stuff it in a jar for a fancy museum!' Bertie continued.

'HA!' spat the General, who appeared to be getting his words back. 'Why would I need to do such a thing? I have publicly renounced the existence of this species and referred to the legend on multiple occasions as "stupid". What have I, me, myself, the accredited General Hornbill, got to prove?'

'General Hornbill might not have anything to prove,' said Kate, joining Bertie on the table, 'but that's not who you are. You're someone who's got *everything* to prove. Tell them, Bertie!'

'You're C. A. Bloom!'

CHAPTER TWENTY

There was a collective gasp.

'*The* C. A. Bloom?!' Captain Mustard's ever-present jolliness vanished in an instant. 'The infamous bird-hoaxer with a controversial methodology?'

'That's him all right!' said Bertie.

'You came aboard my boat to STEAL BIRDS?' The Captain snatched the trophy from C. A. Bloom's white hands.

'I-I-I . . .' General Hornbill flustered.

'Your moustache was always suspiciously impressive!' shouted Dad.

'I'm done with your bullying ways!' Bertie's voice rang out clearly over the crowd. 'I've learned what it means to be a *real* explorer. And this –' he grabbed his Bird Brigading badge and ripped it off – 'isn't it!'

Although most of the crowd had absolutely no idea what was happening, they began to cheer for Bertie.

'Being a Bird Brigader should be fun! We're learning about the wild, after all!'

'Here, here!' said another of the Bird Brigaders. 'All I've done this year is get incredibly strong arm muscles and learn Latin!'

The crowd went wild as, one after another, members of the Bird Brigade rolled their catching jars across the deck and threw their heavy books overboard.

Just when it seemed General Hornbill could go no paler, no more stunned, staggered or dumbfounded –

CA-CAAAAAWWW!

A great shadow swept across the deck. Kate looked up and thought she saw a glimpse of something silky, before something warm and runny was slapped straight on top of her head.

And then it began. Cheers turned to screams and yells as globs of poo fell from the sky like rain. They smattered and pattered and slopped and battered over everything — on top of cakes, shrimps, over frilly tablecloths, slapping straight into the faces of passengers as they stood frozen by the beauty and horror of this glossily plumaged airborne attack.

People threw their hands over their heads and ran for cover. Miss Frou-Frou slipped on a particularly slimy poo, hitting the most impressive

note of her career (a high E) as she fell.

She wasn't the only one – people everywhere were sliding and slithering left and right, fancy dresses and khakis alike smeared with stinking green blobs.
A poop deck it most certainly was.

'Where's the General?' yelled Kate to Rupert, who was hopping from foot to foot in order to dodge the runny bullets.

But she needn't have worried. He was being lifted up, up into the golden jungle sky by three birds. Three birds wearing silky bandanas (which, in the daylight, were clearly made from stolen sleeping bags).

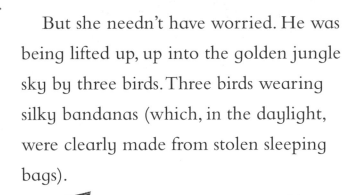

'Put me DOWN!' he was demanding. 'Do you know who I AM?!'

'Hey, Clarence!' Bertie called. Kate saw C. A. Bloom look down from high above the boat. And then Bertie did something magnificent.

He turned around, squatted down and waggled his bare caboose over the edge of the boat at General Hornbill, just because he could.

CHAPTER TWENTY-ONE

It took a long time to clear up all the
poo, but as they mopped and polished
they gave *Miss Custard* the deep clean
she deserved, and she was soon sparkling
in the sun. It was quickly revealed that
Dad was, of course, the real winner of the
Champion-Shrimps, and that Kate had
swapped his name for C. A. Bloom's at the
last minute.

Kate looked out over the jungle. 'I

suppose C. A. Bloom finally got what he wanted – he's as close to the silver wibbler as he can possibly get.'

'But it's on their terms this time,' smiled Rupert, who had tied sponges to his feet and was skating around in delicate circles.

'Did you know, my sweet,' said Dad, mopping his brow and turning to Kate, 'that Catherine Rodríguez has been after C. A. Bloom for years?'

'*What?!*' Kate dropped her mop. 'Why didn't you tell me this earlier?!'

'Well, we didn't know he was him, did we, my love? Look.' Dad handed Kate her most prized possession,

EXAMPLES:

NOTE MY USE OF THE MECHANICAL "GOLDEN WIBBLER" TO ENGROSS FEARED NATURALIST C.A. BLOOM & THUS SNATCH HIS POISONOUS INVENTION

FIG 1

SPEED, NOISE, A SUDDEN PLUNGE IN. "LNESC. 4YT"

The Special Correspondent Manual.

'Catherine Rodríguez was the one to report on The Hoax all those years ago. I remember the day *very* well.' Dad's eyes misted over. 'Your mother and I were picnicking on local cheeses in the Austrian hills . . .'

But Kate wasn't listening. She had just helped Catherine Rodríguez, her One True Idol, get to the bottom of a hugely important story! Could it be that Catherine Rodríguez had known what she was doing when she sent Kate to report on . . .

MORE SHRIIIIMP?!?

Dear Kate,

Well done on another excellent article.

As you've probably worked out, I had my suspicions the infamous C.A. Bloom might be aboard *Miss Custard*, and I did send you there for more than the shrimp.

You've shown curiosity, bravery, and are proving you have all the ingredients needed to make a top-notch Special Correspondent. You have also learned that not every story is yours to tell.

Yours sincerely,

Catherine Rodríguez

Somewhere in the city.

The
END

BIRD BRIGADE SONGS

To chant when walking through the jungle, but to immediately cease when near a potential feathery find.

We're on the Hunt

We're on the hunt for a big, big bird
With a boat-sized bill and a song unheard
With a blue-spotted breast and an eight-foot wing
And if we can't see it we'll hear it sing.

LA LA LA LA LA it goes
LA LA LA LA LA

LA LA LA LA LA it goes
LA LA LA LA LA.
We're on the hunt for a small, small bird
With a silvery song, sleeping undisturbed
With a soft little warble and a half-foot wing
And if we can't see it we'll hear it sing.

CHEEP CHEEP CHEEP CHEEP
    CHEEP it goes
CHEEP CHEEP CHEEP CHEEP
    CHEEP
CHEEP CHEEP CHEEP CHEEP
    CHEEP it goes
    CHEEP CHEEP CHEEP CHEEP
      CHEEP.

The Acronym Song

B is for being the Best (of the best!)
I is for Imagination (Don't use it!)
R is for brigading so hard we don't Rest (No!)
D is for Dehydration! (We're fine!)

B is for a Baited trap to catch the
*R*omping Rook
I is for Impeccable handwriting in our bird-books
G is for the Greeby-sneeb
*A*nd all its flagrant pomp. For the perfect
*D*abbling Dove we trek across this
*E*ndless smelly swamp!

We Are the Bird Brigade

We are the Bird Brigade
To us it's plain to see
That in every glade
Lies a discovery

That the world is full of things
To classify and label
We've got no time, no song or rhyme
For fantasy and fable
We annotate, we contemplate,
Identify and place
For the perfect place to keep a bird
Is stuffed and on a bookcase.

Have you read...

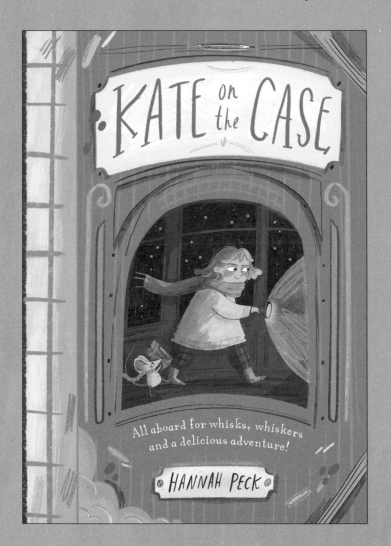

KATE on the CASE

All aboard for whisks, whiskers
and a delicious adventure!

HANNAH PECK

KATE on the CASE

Mystery on the Arctic Express!

Kate and her mouse Rupert have tickets
for the train to the Arctic. But no sooner do they
depart than mysterious things start happening.

Valuable trophies go missing . . .
Ancient scrolls disappear . . .
And a packet of ginger nuts is stolen . . .

Reporter-in-training Kate and Rupert set out to
investigate the colourful cast of suspects, including
the haughty Madame Maude and her cantankerous
cat. But the truth is more
surprising – and
delicious – than they could
have imagined.

This exciting adventure,
wonderfully illustrated
by the author, is
a delightful treat.

Thank you for choosing a Piccadilly Press book.

If you would like to know more about our authors, our books or if you'd just like to know what we're up to, you can find us online.

www.piccadillypress.co.uk

And you can also find us on:

We hope to see you soon!